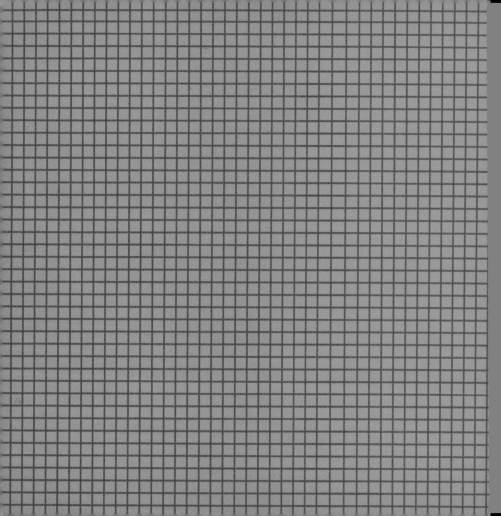

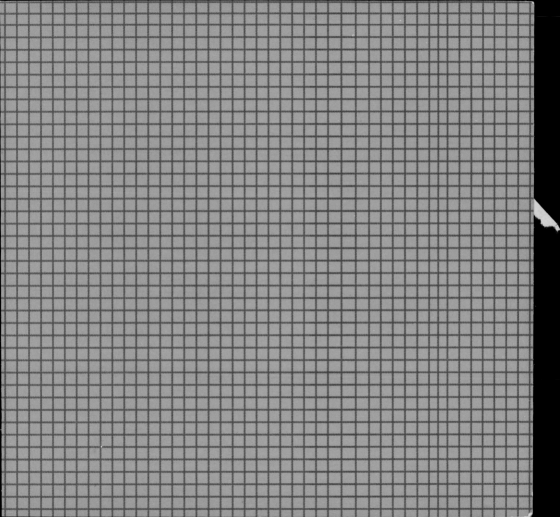

EGMONT

We bring stories to life

First published in Great Britain 2013
This edition published 2015 by Egmont UK Limited,
The Yellow Building, 1 Nicholas Road,
London W11 4AN

HiT entertainment

ISBN 978 0 6035 7159 6
58982/1
Printed in China

Runaway Train

One morning, Station Officer Steele asked Elvis to make him a cup of tea in his special mug.

"No problem, Sir!" said Elvis. "I'll bring it to your office when it's ready."

But while he waited for the kettle to boil, Elvis knocked the mug off the table. It smashed into tiny pieces!

"Oh no!" cried Elvis.

Meanwhile, at the Wholefish Café, Bronwyn had made Gareth some lunch.

Nipper sniffed at the package.

"**Down, boy,**" laughed Gareth. "Come on. I need to get the Pontypandy Flyer ready for action. I'm taking the children up the mountain today."

"I can't wait," said Mandy, excitedly!

Back at the Fire Station, Elvis was in a sticky mess. He had tried to glue the mug back together, and now there was glue everywhere!

"**Where's that tea?**" called Station Officer Steele from his office.

"Erm … coming, Sir," said Elvis, rubbing his sticky hands on his bottom.

Station Officer Steele marched into the room and saw his broken mug. **"Cridlington!"** he growled.

Elvis leapt to his feet, but the chair was stuck to his bottom!

"Oh no! I've glued myself to the chair!" cried Elvis.

"I'll pull you free," said Officer Steele, grabbing the chair. But the chair was covered in glue. Now Officer Steele was stuck too!

Meanwhile, Gareth had arrived at the train station. He hung his lunch bag on the brake lever in the train driver's cab.

Soon the platform was full of people waiting to go on the train.

"**All aboard!**" called Gareth.

"How exciting," said Mrs Chen.

"**Boring,** more like," moaned Norman.

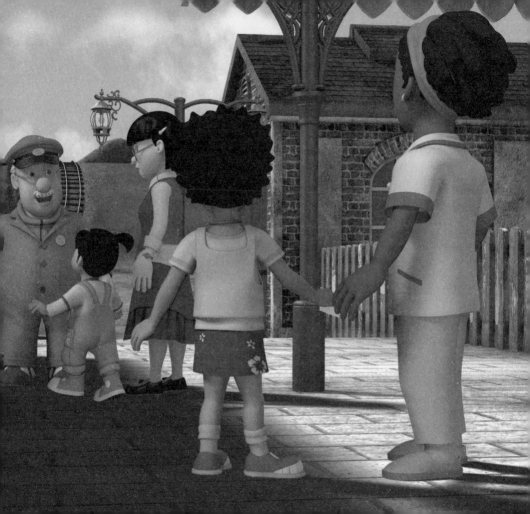

Gareth suddenly remembered he'd left his flask of tea on the platform. He ran off the train to get it.

While Gareth was gone, Nipper crept into the cab. He tugged and tugged at Gareth's lunch bag until ... **CLUNK!** The brake was released.

The train puffed out of the station ... without a driver!

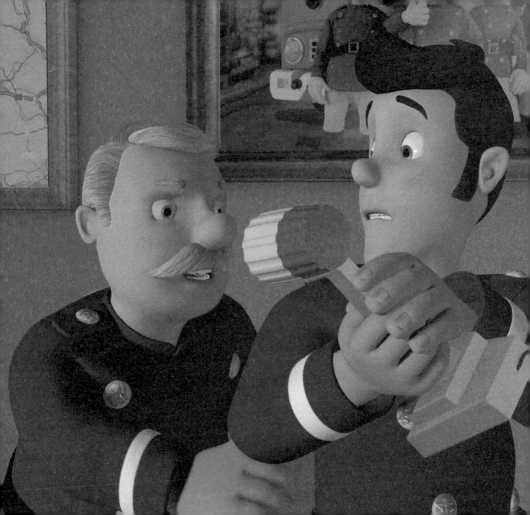

Gareth quickly made
an emergency call to
the Fire Station.

Elvis and Officer Steele
were still stuck to the chair but
they managed to waddle over to take the message.

Then Elvis held the microphone as Officer Steele
put out a call to Fireman Sam and Tom Thomas.

Fireman Sam and Tom jumped into Wallaby One and flew to the Railway Station.

"You have to stop the train before it hits the buffers at the end of the line!" said Gareth.

"We don't have much time," said Tom. **"Let's go, Sam!"**

As the runaway train steamed up the mountain, Norman noticed that the cab was empty.

"We don't have a driver!" said Norman. "**Brilliant!**"

"Look! Someone's swinging from Tom's helicopter," said Mandy.

"**It's Fireman Sam! Cool,**" said Norman.

Fireman Sam landed on top of the carriage
and raced towards the cab. He jumped
through the open window and
pulled on the brake.

The train screeched to a halt – just in time!

"Hooray for Fireman Sam!" cried Mandy.

"Awesome," smiled Norman.

Back at the Fire Station, Officer Steele and Elvis were still in a pickle. "You all right, Sir?" asked Fireman Sam.

"Err, I was demonstrating how firefighters should stick together," said Officer Steele, "and now we're rather stuck to this chair. Can you unstick us, Sam?"

Fireman Sam and Penny laughed so much, they almost fell on the floor!

"I won't forget this sight in a hurry," chuckled Fireman Sam.

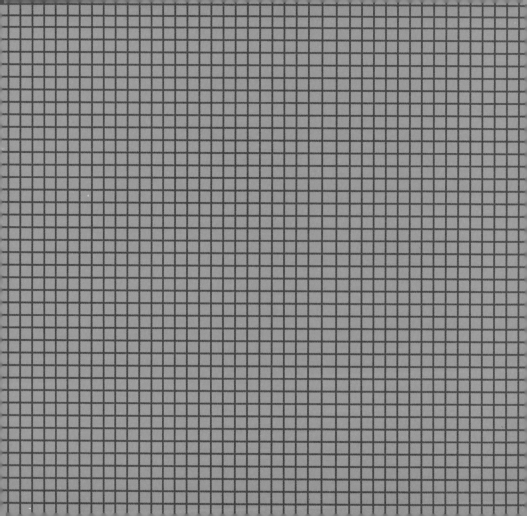

The End

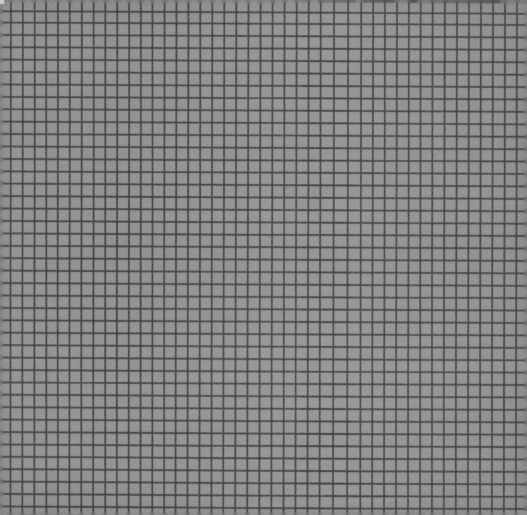

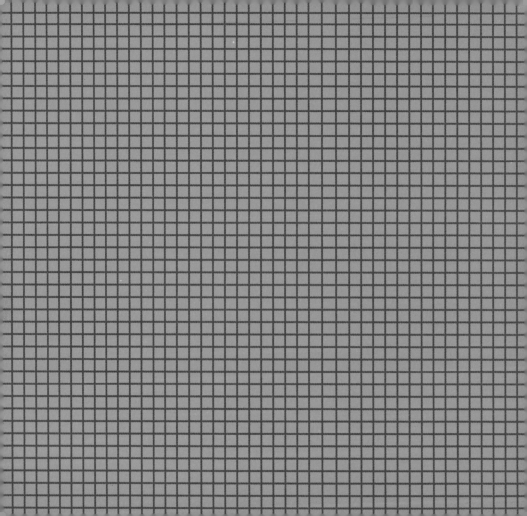